FRANKIE VS. THE KNIGHT'S NASTIES

ALSO BY FRANK LAMPARD

FRANKIE VS. THE KNIGHT'S NASTIES

FRANK LAMPARD

SCHOLASTIC INC.

All rights reserved. Published by Scholastic Inc., 557 Broadway, New York, New York 10012, *Publishers since 1920*. SCHOLASTIC and associated logos are trademarks and/or registered trademarks of Scholastic Inc. Published by arrangement with Little, Brown Books for Young Readers.

The publisher does not have any control over and does not assume any responsibility for author or third-party websites or their content.

This book is a work of fiction. Names, characters, places, and incidents are either the product of the author's imagination or are used fictitiously, and any resemblance to actual persons, living or dead, business establishments, events, or locales is entirely coincidental.

ISBN 978-1-338-08907-3

10 9 8 7 6 5 4 3 2 1   16 17 18 19 20

Printed in the U.S.A.   40
First printing 2016

*To my mom, Pat, who encouraged
me to do my homework in
between kicking a ball all around
the house, and is still with me
every step of the way.*

Welcome to a fantastic
fantasy league—the greatest
soccer competition ever held
in this world or any other!

You'll need four on a team,
so choose carefully. This is a lot
more serious than a game in the
park. You'll never know who your
next opponents will be, or
where you'll face them.

So lace up your cleats, players,
and good luck! The whistle's
about to blow!

The Ref

CHAPTER 1

Brrriiing!

The bell rang at the end of the period. All week Mr. Donald had been teaching Frankie's class about the Middle Ages—knights and castles and tournaments. Frankie had loved every minute.

"Good job, class!" said Mr.

Donald. "Tomorrow we'll be looking at each other's projects."

"Oh no!" said Louise. "We haven't finished ours."

Frankie looked down at the model castle in front of them, with its battlements made of egg cartons and its moat from blue tissue paper. Its cardboard towers still needed to be painted, and they hadn't stuck the flags to the turrets yet.

The class had split up into groups of three to make their projects, so Frankie had joined his friends Louise and Charlie. Another team— led by Kobe—had decorated a

wooden shield with a coat of
arms, while Tanya's group had
put together a book of medieval
recipes. Pablo and his friends had
wanted to make a papier-mâché
dragon, but Mr. Donald had said
that dragons weren't real, so they
settled instead on putting together

a miniature catapult that fired Ping-Pong balls.

And they had *all* finished. One by one the class filed out.

Frankie raised his hand. "Can we just have ten more minutes?"

Mr. Donald looked at his watch. "Of course you can. But stay out of trouble!"

He picked up his briefcase and left the classroom as well.

Charlie was trying to put glue on one of the flagpoles, which were made from old lollipop sticks. But so far he hadn't been very successful. His goalie gloves were making him clumsy.

"Why don't you take them off?" asked Louise.

"Gotta stay ready," Charlie replied without looking up.

He finally managed to put a flagpole in place.

"Right," said Frankie. "Let's all get painting."

Frankie went to the back of the classroom to get the paint tubes. His ankle was sore from where he'd twisted it in a tackle the week before. He hoped it was going to get better because his school was playing Ryles Park this weekend.

As he got the paints, Frankie

heard a knock at the classroom door. His older brother, Kevin, peered in, grinning. *Great!* thought Frankie. *This is all we need!*

"What are you still doing here?" Kevin said. "The bell rang a couple of minutes ago."

"We're finishing our project," said Charlie, gesturing to the castle with his glove.

Kevin sniggered. "What a bunch of geeks." He strode into the room and grabbed Frankie's bag, then started rooting around inside.

"Hey!" said Frankie.

"I need your house keys," he said. "I lost mine." He tipped the bag upside down and all of Frankie's stuff fell out. His books, his pencil case, his lunchbox. And his battered soccer ball.

Frankie fished in his pocket and took out his keys. "They're *here*!" he said. "Why didn't you just ask nicely?"

Kevin grunted and tossed the bag aside. He snatched the keys from Frankie's hand.

"Don't stay too late, teacher's pets," he said and marched back toward the door.

On the way, he saw the soccer ball. Drawing back his foot, he smashed the ball against the whiteboard. Frankie watched in horror as it bounced off. Everything seemed to happen in slow motion. The ball looped through the air, right toward their model castle. Louise's mouth became a perfect "O" shape. Charlie dropped the glue and reached out, but Frankie could see it was too late. The ball smacked straight down onto the delicate construction, crushing it completely.

"What have you done?" said Frankie.

His brother did look a little bit worried for a second. Then he shrugged, said "Oops!", and rushed out of the classroom.

Frankie, Charlie, and Louise gathered around the remains of their project. The soccer ball sat on top of the shattered towers like a giant cannonball.

"It's not fair," said Louise.

"Don't worry," said Charlie, putting a gloved hand on her shoulder. "We can fix it."

"It was hours of work!" said Frankie. First his ankle, now this. It was turning into a rotten week.

Suddenly, the air seemed to vibrate. The soccer ball wobbled. A grin spread over Frankie's face. The soccer ball began to sink into the ground, then more of the ground

beneath their feet slipped away into
an ever-widening hole. But instead
of earth below, he saw swirling
colors, like a giant rainbow chute in
the classroom floor.

His feet slipped out from beneath
him and he tumbled into the hole.

The chute was like the best
slide he'd ever been on, and he felt
almost weightless as he plunged
straight down.

"Wheeeee!" yelled Charlie.

The slide changed direction,
lurching sideways. Frankie spun
onto his back and hurtled headfirst.
Then the tunnel seemed to be
traveling *upward*. He felt himself

slowing down. The colors ahead
vanished into blackness. For a
split second, fear gripped him.
What if it was a dead end this
time? They might all get squished,
or lost forever in some dark
underworld.

As he shot into the unknown, he
clamped his eyes shut . . .

CHAPTER 2

Frankie felt solid ground beneath
his feet and a light breeze stirring
his hair.

He opened his eyes, and his
breath caught in his throat.

He and the others were standing
in a field of short grass. Charlie
was wearing a white ruffled shirt

and a leather waistcoat, with skin–tight leggings and soft shoes like slippers. Frankie himself had a red tunic tied loosely with a belt, and leather boots. Louise was gasping at her satin dress that trailed right down to the ground. "Not again—I *hate* dresses!" she said.

Frankie gasped as he saw the grand–looking castle behind them.

At the front of the castle was a tall metal gate with an open drawbridge over a moat.

"No way!" said Charlie.

"Yes way," said Louise. "We're in the Middle Ages!"

They all heard a squeal and turned to see Max, Frankie's dog, rolling in the grass. The soccer ball's magic always brought the whole team, even if they weren't together. And Max could always talk in these worlds! Max got up and looked around.

"Not *again*!" He sighed. "I was just about to chase the neighbor's cat out of the yard at home, and then everything went topsy-turvy."

Frankie smiled. He knew Max was terrified of Panther, the black cat who lived next door.

"We must be here to play a game," said Louise.

Frankie tensed, suddenly worried. *What about my injured ankle?*

Thunder rumbled in the distance.

"That's weird," said Charlie, looking up. "There isn't a single cloud in the sky."

He was right. The sky was clear blue.

The thunder rumbled closer.

"Er . . . I don't think that's a storm," said Louise, her face pale. "It's coming from the ground."

Frankie felt it through his legs. The whole field beneath his feet seemed to be trembling. He laid his hand on the grass, just to be

18

sure. "Maybe it's an earthquake," he said.

Then he looked up and saw the horrible truth. Across the field, a line of twenty horses was galloping toward them. On each rode a knight in gleaming armor, staring from behind steel helmets and clutching long swords.

"They can't be charging at us, can they?" mumbled Charlie.

The horses were getting closer, covering the ground at breakneck speed, churning up mud and grass with their hooves. They showed no signs of slowing down.

"I think so!" said Louise.

Frankie pointed to the castle and yelled to his friends. "RUN!"

Max darted off ahead, his short legs a blur. Charlie and Louise sprinted after him. Frankie winced as pain shot through his ankle, but he gritted his teeth and ran as fast as he could toward the drawbridge. Casting desperate glances over his shoulder, he saw the knights closing in fast.

Max crossed the drawbridge first. Frankie saw soldiers inside, rushing around in panic. He heard the cry, "Raise the drawbridge! We're being attacked!"

Louise and Charlie ran onto the bridge, twenty feet ahead of Frankie. He pumped his arms for extra speed. The chains on either side of the drawbridge went taut. To his horror, it began to rise.

Charlie and Louise stood at the edge. "Run, Frankie!" they cried.

As Frankie hurtled toward them, the drawbridge creaked upward.

I'm not going to make it, he thought. *I'm going to get stuck on this side and get trampled!*

He was ten feet from the drawbridge, but already it was at head-height.

"Jump, Frankie!" shouted Charlie, reaching out his hands.

Frankie didn't have time to think. *It's jump or nothing.* The moat opened up below, the waters dark. Frankie took a deep, ragged breath and pushed off from his good foot, stretching up his arms.

I'm not going to make it . . . He felt himself falling . . .

Gloved hands grabbed his wrists

and Frankie was suddenly swinging in the air.

"Got you!" said Charlie.

Frankie looked up and saw Louise leaning over, too. She managed to grip his tunic and together his two friends heaved him over the edge of the drawbridge. They tumbled over the rough timbers as it creaked higher.

Frankie landed in a heap at the bottom, the wind knocked out of his lungs. Charlie sprawled over him. They untangled themselves from each other as the drawbridge slammed closed.

"Phew!" said Louise, rubbing her head. "I think we're safe."

"Far from it," said a gruff voice. Frankie turned and saw three soldiers in dented armor. They pointed long pikes at Frankie and his friends.

"Prince Arthur doesn't look kindly on trespassers," said one soldier. "On your feet!"

Frankie and his friends got up slowly. "We're not trespassers," he said. "I can explain."

"Oh yes?" said the soldier.

Frankie glanced at his friends and realized that actually he couldn't explain at all. *They probably don't believe in magic soccer balls!*

"Well . . . " he began. "It's not exactly simple . . . "

"Let's see what the prince wants to do with the prisoners," said the lead soldier. "Where'd that mutt get to?"

"Dunno," said another, "but what harm can a little dog do? With any luck, Cook will find him and put him in a stew. I haven't had meat for weeks."

Frankie drew a sharp breath. *I hope they're joking.*

One of the soldiers gave him a shove in the back. "Move it!" he said.

They were marched across a courtyard, past a stable where several horses watched over stall

doors. Pigs and chickens ran
across their path and a few people
dressed in filthy clothes stared.
Smoke rose from what looked like a
blacksmith's forge. A bare-chested
man inside used a hammer to beat a
piece of glowing hot metal.

He's making a sword! Frankie
realized.

Frankie's ankle was throbbing
as they climbed some steps to
a set of double doors. The lead
soldier pushed through and right
away Frankie heard raucous shouts
coming from inside. They entered
a grand chamber. A huge circular
table filled the room. Around it

men were sitting looking at a map of the castle and the surroundings. Tapestries hung on the wall, showing battle scenes, and even what looked like a soccer game.

No way! thought Frankie. Mr. Donald said they didn't play soccer in the Middle Ages.

As the knights turned one by one to look at the new arrivals, they fell silent.

"Your Highness!" bellowed the soldier. "We caught these intruders sneaking into the castle on behalf of Prince Egbert!"

At the far side of the table, a young man stood up. He couldn't

have been much older than fifteen.
Frankie noticed that while the
other knights sat on stools wearing
armor, he was dressed in fine red
and green velvet and sat on a tall
throne. *He must be Prince Arthur.*

"Wait a minute," said Louise. "We
don't even know who Prince Egbert
is!"

"Silence!" shouted a huge knight
sitting beside the prince. He had a
black mustache that matched his
coal-black eyes.

"And if we were *sneaking*,"
added Charlie, "we'd hardly come in
through the front door!"

The knight glowered. "I'll take

them to the dungeons." He turned
to the prince and bowed. "If that's
your wish, Your Highness."

Prince Arthur nodded meekly
and whispered, "As Sir Winalot
commands."

CHAPTER 3

This isn't going very well, thought Frankie as they were led back across the courtyard toward a low dark doorway. Sir Winalot strode ahead of them.

"I hope you like rats," he said. "Because the ones down there are *very* friendly."

Something shot through the air
and crunched into the wall above
their heads. Shards of stone rained
down.

Everyone stopped, staring as the
dust settled.

Then another object—a boulder
the size of a soccer ball—arced
overhead. It smashed into the
blacksmith's forge, knocking a hole
in the roof. Sparks flew from inside
as the blacksmith ran away. Chickens
squawked and scattered.

Sir Winalot turned to Frankie,
his eyes wide. Then he opened his
mouth in a mighty bellow. "We're
being attacked!"

A wave of panic spread across the castle as more lumps of stone flew over the battlements.

Wait a minute, thought Frankie. *They aren't just the size of soccer balls . . . they* are *soccer balls!*

Frankie ducked down against a wall. Sir Winalot strode into the center of the courtyard, drawing his sword and pulling down the visor of his helmet. "Archers to positions!"

A stone soccer ball arced over the wall, heading straight for him. The knight saw it coming but seemed rooted to the spot. Charlie sprinted across the courtyard and barreled into him. As the soccer ball slammed into the ground, they both went tumbling.

Sir Winalot gaped, as if he didn't understand what had happened. Then he glanced skyward, his eyes goggling.

Frankie looked up as well and his stomach turned to jelly. A jet of fire blasted against the castle wall. He couldn't make sense of what he was seeing. Two enormous scaly wings beating up and down. A black body, at least twenty feet long with spikes jutting from a ridged back.

"Dragons aren't real," he mumbled.

But this one was. It dipped its

long head and swooped down into
the courtyard, straight toward
Frankie. As it flew at him he saw its
jaws open, revealing black teeth like
splinters of charred wood. Frankie
backed away and stumbled over a
stone soccer ball. He saw the red
glow of fire building in the depths

of the dragon's throat. The monster settled its golden eyes on him and Frankie knew he was about to get blasted with flame.

He slipped a toe beneath the stone soccer ball and flicked it upward. It looped right into the dragon's mouth. The flames died in an instant. With a choking sound, the dragon backed away, flapping its leathery wings in panic. Smoke billowed from its flaring nostrils.

The dragon flew back over the castle walls, still shaking its head to dislodge the ball. At once, the bombardment ceased. Soldiers were running with buckets of

sloshing water to put out the
flames. Others were peering out
from doorways to see if it was safe.

Sir Winalot was climbing a
set of stairs, leading up to the
battlements. Frankie ran after him,
with Louise and Charlie following.

"I told you we weren't the
enemy," Frankie called after the
knight.

At the top of the stairs, Sir
Winalot glared out from the walls.
Frankie gasped when he saw what
lay below. Where there had been
just a field, now there were dozens
of tents with horses tied up outside
and men in armor milling around.

There were wooden towers on wheels for scaling walls, a battering ram made from a mighty tree trunk, and giant catapults.

Sir Winalot laid one of his gauntlets on the turret. "Prince Egbert is a fool. No amount of stone soccer balls can knock down these walls."

"But what if he lays siege?" said Louise. "You won't be able to get food into the castle and we'll all starve!"

Sir Winalot sniffed, looking annoyed. He obviously hadn't thought of that.

As they watched, a lone rider

cantered toward the castle. He wasn't a knight in armor. From his black clothes, Frankie recognized him at once.

"That's the Ref!" he said. "What's he doing on their side?"

The rider stopped beneath the walls and unrolled a scroll tucked in his belt. His voice carried up to them.

"This is a message for Prince Arthur from his brother!" he called. "Hand over the castle to its rightful owner, Prince Egbert. Or else!"

"Never!" cried Sir Winalot.

"Then you will all go hungry!" said the Ref. He turned his horse and began to ride away.

We can't let this knight's stubbornness get us all killed, thought Frankie.

"Wait!" he shouted.

The Ref stopped.

"What are you doing, boy?" asked Sir Winalot.

"Let's settle this another way," shouted Frankie. "With a tournament!" Even Louise and Charlie were looking at him strangely. "Trust me," he said.

"A tournament?" called the Ref. "Jousting?"

"No," replied Frankie. "A soccer game!"

He thought he saw the Ref grin.

"So be it!" the Ref said.
"Tomorrow, an hour after dawn,
have your team ready! A soccer
game will decide the castle's
fate."

Sir Winalot narrowed his eyes
and gave Frankie a hard slap
between the shoulder blades.
"Good thinking, boy."

Frankie blushed. It looked like he
was finally winning over the scary
knight.

"Where can we practice?" asked
Frankie.

Sir Winalot's smile faded. "You?"
he said, puffing out his chest. "I'm
the captain of Prince Arthur's team.

You kiddies wouldn't even make the
subs bench! Anyway, I've got other
plans for you."

As he strode away, Frankie's
hopes of ever getting home faded.

CHAPTER 4

A feast was called to celebrate the upcoming match. According to Sir Winalot, his team of knights were the best players in the land. The question of which brother owned the castle would be settled once and for all.

Everyone was in a good mood.

Everyone except for Frankie and his friends. They were working as servants. Frankie was running up and down stairs, bringing food from the kitchen. Louise was serving drinks from a jug, and Charlie had been dressed as a jester. He was doing his best to juggle flaming torches. His gloves were coming in handy.

At least we were spared the dungeon, thought Frankie.

Frankie took a platter of roasted chicken legs to Prince Arthur. Actually, he didn't look happy, either. Frankie bowed as he held out the food.

"You don't have to do that," said Prince Arthur, taking a leg and gnawing on it.

Frankie straightened. It was the first time the prince had spoken to him.

"How come you aren't joining in the celebrations like the rest of them?"

Frankie asked, nodding to where Sir Winalot and his burly knights were loudly singing a soccer song.

"What's to celebrate? I just wish my brother Egbert wasn't such a brute," he said. "We used to get along when we were younger."

Frankie nodded. He remembered a time when he and Kevin used to be friends, too.

"But he changed," continued Arthur. "He became nasty and mean. That's why my father left me the castle rather than Egbert, even though I'm younger. He thought I'd be a better leader."

"At least this soccer game will

settle things once and for all," said Frankie.

"You think so?" Arthur replied, shaking his head. "Even if we win, he'll just attack again. He won't stop until the castle's a ruin."

"Hey, boy!" shouted Sir Winalot to Frankie. "More food."

Frankie left Prince Arthur slouched in his chair and headed to the kitchen. The heat rose up from the ovens and servants ran sweating in the torch-lit gloom. Frankie headed for a long table where more trays of food waited. Before he got there, a beautiful young woman with golden hair approached with a plate of cakes.

"Take these!" she said. "With the best wishes of the cook to Sir Winalot's team."

Frankie took the plate and picked up a platter of roasted lamb legs as well. Balancing them carefully, he headed up the stairs.

He gave the cakes to Sir Winalot, whose teammates devoured them in seconds. He was about to place the lamb on the table when he felt something brush his leg. It was Max. The dog ducked back under the table.

"Where've you been?" muttered Frankie.

"Staying out of harm's way," said Max. His nostrils twitched. "Is that lamb?"

"You can't have any!" said Frankie.

"Couldn't you accidentally drop a bit?" said Max.

At home, Frankie's dad called Max "The Hoover" because he ate anything that hit the floor. Frankie checked that no one was looking and threw a piece of lamb beneath the table.

"Stay out of sight," he said. "We've got to find a way out of here."

But looking at Sir Winalot and his team, food flecked over their clothes and cheeks flushed, he couldn't see much hope at all.

A cry went up from the other side of the hall. Flames were licking up one of the wall tapestries.

"It was an accident!" said Charlie. He'd obviously dropped one of the torches.

Louise rushed over and emptied a whole pitcher over the flames. They sizzled to nothing.

"Hey!" bellowed Sir Winalot.

"Maybe you should all get a decent night's sleep," snapped Louise. "You might play better."

All the knights shot to their feet, shouting angrily. One picked up a loaf of bread and hurled it at Louise. She took it on the chest, then on her knee, and head-butted it back to Charlie. He head-butted it to Frankie. Without thinking, Frankie volleyed it. It whizzed right past Sir Winalot's head and hit the wall.

The huge knight looked furious. His hand went to the hilt of his sword and he drew the blade a few inches.

"Enough!" said Prince Arthur. "The girl is right, Sir Winalot. It's time for you and your team to rest."

Sir Winalot slid his sword back into its scabbard and stormed out

of the chamber, followed by his knights.

As the doors slammed behind him, Frankie saw Max munching on the lamb bone.

"He's grumpier than your dad on Monday mornings," said the dog.

"You should sleep, too," said Prince Arthur as he flopped back onto his throne. "If we lose the match tomorrow, tonight might be our last taste of freedom."

CHAPTER 5

Frankie and his friends were
given an empty stall in the stables
with straw to sleep on. But
with Charlie's snoring, Louise's
fidgeting, and Max's paws wheeling
in his dreams, Frankie didn't get
much sleep. The same thoughts ran
through his mind. *If Sir Winalot's*

*team loses, are we stuck here? And
if they win, what does that mean?
Will we be allowed to go home?*

Frankie was even starting to miss
Kevin, so he knew it must be bad.

He rubbed his eyes as the first
rays of sun peeped through the
stall door.

Walking out of the stables, Frankie
went to the well to splash his face
with water. All was quiet, until . . .

"BLEUUUURGH!"

The sound of someone retching
echoed around the courtyard,
followed by a groan.

Frankie followed the noise. It
was coming from the main chamber

where the feast had taken place. Max joined him, scampering at his heel.

"Did you hear that, too?" Frankie said.

Max barked. "It sounds like someone being sick."

Behind the doors they found Sir Winalot bent over, clutching his stomach. By the look of it, he'd already emptied most of its contents onto one of the tapestries. The rest of his team was sitting on the floor, looking distinctly green in the face. Prince Arthur looked very glum. "What are we going to do?"

Another knight was groaning in the corner.

Louise arrived, too, with Charlie.
"Not enough rest," she said, folding
her arms.

Sir Winalot stumbled over to
a chair and sank onto it. "It's not
that," he said. He nodded to a tall
knight with a wet cloth over his
head. "Sir Safehands went to bed

early, but he's just as ill. It must have been the food."

"But everyone ate the food," said Charlie.

Frankie had a sinking feeling as he remembered the beautiful woman in the kitchen.

"The cakes," he muttered.

"What's that?" snapped Sir Winalot.

Frankie explained about the golden-haired woman, and the plate of cakes baked by the cook especially for the team.

"Poison?" said Louise.

"This sounds like the Crone's trickery!" said Sir Safehands.

"The who?" said Frankie.

"The Crone is a witch, a sorceress who works for my brother," said Arthur. "She can change her appearance with magic."

"As *well* you know," said Sir Winalot, stabbing a finger toward Frankie. He bent over, coughing. "I *knew* these strangers were working for Egbert. Off with their heads, I say!"

Soldiers by the door stepped forward to seize Frankie and his friends.

"Wait!" Frankie said. "Don't you see? We're your only hope."

"What do you mean?" said Prince
Arthur.

The soldiers closed in.

"Your team is out of action,"
said Frankie. "You need players to
face Prince Egbert's side. Let us
stand in."

Sir Winalot wiped his mouth.
"No! You won't steal my glory!"

"You don't look very glorious at
the moment," said Louise. "I don't
think any of you could even kick a
ball in the state you're in."

One of the soldiers grabbed
Frankie's arms, but he managed to
wriggle free.

"Let us at least try," he said. "If

we lose—"he glanced at Louise and Charlie—"then you can do what you like."

Prince Arthur pressed his lips together as if considering his options. Finally, he nodded. "So be it. You will be our champions at the tournament."

"And if you fail, it's the headsman's axe for you," grumbled Sir Winalot.

Charlie ran up to Frankie. "Are you sure about this? I quite like my head where it is."

Frankie looked his friend in the eyes. "Then we'd better not lose."

*

As the drawbridge was lowered, Frankie's heart began to thump like a drum.

Boom! Boom! Boom!

Then he realized that there *was* a drum, beating in the camp ahead of them.

The tents had been rearranged in a rectangle in the shape of a field. Egbert's soldiers stood in two columns, making a path between them. Prince Arthur led the way on his horse, with Sir Winalot riding at his side. He had his helmet visor down so no one could see how green his face was. Frankie followed on foot with Charlie, Louise, and Max.

The soldiers watched them, snarling and spitting.

As they reached the field, with goalposts set up at either end, Frankie saw a large tent opposite flying a black flag. The Ref stepped into the center, holding a soccer ball. "Where is your team?" he asked.

Prince Arthur waved a hand toward Frankie and his friends. "Frankie's FC will play for me."

The crowd burst into laughter.

"This is going to be *messy*," Frankie heard.

The Ref lifted a whistle to his lips and blew.

AYOOOOO!

The flaps of the large tent parted and out walked a thin boy, tall and standing very straight, chin lifted proudly. Frankie could see from the shape of his face that he was Arthur's brother, Egbert. Next came an old woman leaning on a staff, her silver hair hanging in knotted tresses over her shoulders.

"She looks harmless enough," said Charlie.

"I'm not harmless," said the woman with a toothless smirk. "Perhaps you haven't heard how powerful my magic is." She lifted up her staff and waved it in front of her face. Her features blurred.

For a moment Frankie saw the beautiful woman from the kitchen again.

"So she's the Crone!" said Max. "She smells rotten."

The Crone hissed at him and pointed a warty finger. "Quiet, little furball, or I'll turn you into a cat!"

Max scuttled behind Frankie's legs.

Behind the elderly lady came a hooded figure, his face concealed under a brown cowl. He looked like a monk. He heard Prince Arthur whisper to Sir Winalot, "Who's that?"

The knight shook his head. "I don't know," he said.

"I think we've got a chance," said Louise. "They don't look that good."

"They've still got one more player to come out," said Charlie.

"Where's Scorcher?" asked Prince Egbert.

Whoosh!

The tent behind him was suddenly ablaze, collapsing to ashes in a few seconds. Inside stood the dragon, looking pleased with himself.

Frankie's mouth went dry. He swallowed thickly.

"Still like our chances?" he asked Louise.

CHAPTER 6

The Ref kicked the ball high into the
air, raised the whistle to his lips,
and let out a blast.

"Let the game begin!"

The watching soldiers roared. As
Charlie rushed to their goal, Louise
ran for the ball while the other
team stood still. *What are they
doing?* wondered Frankie.

Louise had almost reached the ball when she tripped and sprawled on to the grass. The spectators laughed.

That's not like Louise, Frankie thought.

She tried to stand and tripped again, peering at her feet.

"My laces!" she said.

Frankie looked closer and saw

that they were tied together. He glanced up and saw the Crone waving her staff and grinning.

"Magic!" he said.

Egbert sprang forward, took the ball, and ran at their goal. Frankie blocked him, but Egbert's legs moved like a blur and he went around Frankie with ease.

That's not right, thought Frankie. *No one's that fast.*

Max tried to tackle him, too, but Egbert trapped the ball between his feet and somersaulted over the top of the dog like a gymnast. He was clear to the goal, with only Charlie to stop him.

Frankie's friend crouched low, his eyes on the ball. Egbert took a shot and the ball screamed toward the goal. Charlie dove the right way.

He's going to stop it, Frankie thought.

Then suddenly, Charlie dropped to the ground, hands first.

The ball hit the back of the net.

Charlie was still trying to get up, but his gloves seemed stuck to the grass.

"They've turned to stone!" he shouted.

Frankie saw the Crone waving her staff once more.

"Ref, that's cheating," he said.

The Ref cocked his head and pulled out a thick book with *Rules of Soccer* written on the front. He quickly flicked through. "Nope," he said. "It doesn't state anywhere that a player can't use magic."

"That's because magic doesn't exist!" said Louise.

"If you say so," said the Ref. "Play on. One-nothing to the Knight's Nasties."

Frankie grimaced. *We need to be smarter than them.* He called his team to him. "The key is to keep it moving," he said. "Pass it before the Crone can work her magic."

Charlie left his stone gloves on the ground and tossed the ball to Frankie. He dribbled it out. From the corner of his eye, he saw the witch pointing her staff. He kicked the ball quickly to Max. "One touch!" Frankie shouted.

Max did as he said, passing it to Louise. A moment after he'd kicked it, a hole appeared in the ground and the dog tumbled in. But now Louise had the ball. As the Crone followed her with her staff, Louise passed it back to Frankie. He heard the witch curse, "Stand still, will you?"

Egbert ran toward Frankie.

"You're in the way!" the Crone yelled at him.

Frankie put on a burst of speed past Egbert, but the prince was just as quick. Frankie back-heeled to Max, who had jumped out of the hole.

The dog ran toward the goal, and Scorcher spread his wings.

"Careful, Max!" shouted Frankie.

Max blasted the ball at the bottom corner of the goal.

"Supergoal!" shouted Frankie.

But just before the ball hit the net, a spurt of flame met it. The ball turned to ash.

"Ref!" barked Max. "You've got

to be kidding. A goalkeeper isn't allowed to breathe fire on the ball."

The Ref took out the rule book and flicked through it again.

"It doesn't say that in here, I'm afraid. Goal kick."

Another ball was thrown on to the field. Scorcher flicked it out with his wing. The Crone lifted her staff and guided it to the feet of the hooded stranger. Frankie was on him in a flash. They shoved each other as they ran, then the stranger gave Frankie a nasty kick on his injured ankle. Frankie crumpled with a cry of pain and watched as his opponent exchanged passes

with Prince Egbert. They went around Louise easily, then rushed at Charlie. Two on one. He had no chance. He threw himself at the ball, but the prince was quicker and passed it just in time.

The hooded player put the ball in the back of the net, then did a silly little wiggle-dance, then a fist-pump.

Frankie frowned. He knew that dance all too well. *But it can't be him . . . That's crazy!*

"Two-nothing to Egbert's team," said the Ref. He blew his whistle for half-time.

Frankie looked back and saw

Prince Arthur with his head in his hands. Sir Winalot was doing his very best glare.

He looks like he's looking forward to chopping off our heads! thought Frankie with a shiver.

He called his team closer, and Louise helped Charlie off the ground. "We've got two problems," she said. "The witch is stopping us from playing, and the dragon won't let us score. We need to deal with both of them. I've got a plan to stop Scorcher, but we'll need help from Prince Arthur and Sir Winalot."

"As long as it doesn't involve me being bait," growled Max.

A smile played over Frankie's lips. "You can help me with the Crone," he said. Louise told him her plan and Frankie shared his idea, too.

"Let me get this straight," said Charlie when they had finished. "You want me to play badly?"

"That's right," said Louise, grinning.

"No one will believe it." Charlie frowned. "I *never* play badly."

"That doesn't matter," said Louise. "Just try!"

"What's the holdup?" called Egbert. "I want my castle back!"

"Ready?" Frankie said to his team. "Let's do this."

CHAPTER 7

No one noticed Sir Winalot
sneaking back to the castle.

The second half started with a
whistle, and Charlie pulled his arm
back to roll the ball out to Louise.
But instead he hurled it right up
over their heads, over the tents and
toward the castle. It rolled into the

moat with a splash, beneath the raised drawbridge.

Perfect, thought Frankie.

"I'm not getting it," said Prince Egbert.

"Well, I'm not either," said the Crone.

The hooded stranger, silent as always, shook his head and pointed to the dragon.

Frankie held his breath. *So far the plan's working.*

Scorcher sighed. "If I must!"

With two wing beats, he lifted off the ground and flew over toward the moat. His massive shadow crossed the fields and then he hovered over the water. He reached down to pluck the ball out with his claws.

"Now!" yelled Louise.

Everyone looked confused.

With a rattling sound, the drawbridge suddenly lowered.

CLUNK!

It dropped right onto Scorcher's head, knocking him into the water with a huge splash. He resurfaced with water pouring off his scales. "Who did that? I'll make them pay!"

Sir Winalot stood in the gatehouse with his hands on the drawbridge lever.

Scorcher turned on the knight,

then drew back his head, jaws
opening. Sir Winalot's knees
trembled in fear.

"Barbecue time!" cackled the
Crone.

But instead of flame, all that
came out of the dragon's mouth
was a smoke ring.

"It worked!" said Louise, high–fiving Frankie. "His flames are doused."

"Get back here and get in goal!" yelled Egbert. "Let's finish this."

By the time Scorcher was back, the Ref had produced another ball. He rolled it to the prince. The Crone waved her staff and Egbert sped off.

She's making him run quicker! Frankie realized. *No wonder we can't catch him. Time to put Plan B into action.*

As Frankie ran after Egbert, he shouted, "Fetch!"

Max, who had been lurking on the sidelines, charged at the Crone.

She was so busy directing magic at Egbert that she didn't see him until he was close. He leapt into the air, mouth gaping, and snatched the staff from her hand, just like it was a stick at the park.

Egbert tripped over his own feet and the ball came to Frankie.

"Now we're even," he said, passing the ball to Louise. She nutmegged the hooded stranger and ran toward the goal. Without his fire, Scorcher looked clumsy. He tried to stop the ball with his wing, but Louise's shot had too much power. The ball buried itself in the net.

"Two-one!" she said.

The crowd groaned. Only Prince Arthur clapped.

Egbert stood up and dusted himself off. He looked at the Crone. "Do something, old woman!"

"I can't," she replied. "That awful dog has my staff."

Max lay on the ground, happily chewing on the piece of wood.

"What about you?" said Egbert, pointing at the hooded stranger.

The cloaked figure just shrugged.

The game restarted. Egbert had the ball, but he was slower than before. Max easily tackled him. This time the hooded stranger was after him. A moment before he lunged in for a tackle, Frankie passed the ball and jumped up. He was sure the stranger was aiming for his injured ankle again, but he slid harmlessly beneath.

The crowd groaned again as Max scored past the fireless dragon.

"Two-all!"

Max and his team stood facing their opponents. Egbert was breathing hard. Without her staff, the Crone was just a tired old woman. The dragon looked distinctly glum. Only the hooded stranger still stood tall. Though Frankie couldn't see his eyes, he felt the hateful glare on him. *It's like he knows about my ankle. But how?*

The game restarted with the Ref's whistle. Once again, Frankie and his team passed it effortlessly around their opponents. "You should score the winner, Captain," said Louise, rolling the ball to Frankie. The dragon had managed to get one wing caught in the net. It was practically an open goal.

Frankie hesitated with the ball at his feet. The crowd was watching, silent.

"Go on!" yelled Prince Arthur. "Finish it like a true champion!"

Frankie thought back to all the goals he'd scored for school. Some of those had won the game, too. He remembered the glorious feeling as the ball flew into the net.

But this doesn't feel like that at all.

The other team was hopeless. They were hardly worth beating.

He turned away from the ball.

"I think we've proved our point," he said.

"You have to play until the final whistle," said the Ref. "Otherwise the game is forfeit to your opponents."

Frankie kicked the ball away. "This game is about who owns that castle," said Frankie, "but I don't think either of them should. They should share it. That's what brothers do."

Charlie, Max, and Louise walked to Frankie's side.

"He's right," said Louise.

"Nonsense!" said Prince Arthur. "It's my castle. I want it. Score the goal! I command you!"

"Play on!" said the Ref.

No one moved. No one apart from the hooded stranger. The ball had rolled close to him, so he kicked it upfield. Charlie had left his goal wide open, thinking the game was over.

The hooded man knocked the ball with his left foot, ready to blast it with his right. As he swung his boot, Prince Egbert slid in, tackling him.

"You idiot!" said the hooded man, in a voice Frankie knew all too well. "We could have won!"

The Ref blew his whistle for the end of the game. "It's a draw!" he shouted. "The castle is therefore shared."

"You'd better still give me my gold," the hooded man was saying. "You promised me gold!"

Frankie stepped forward, grabbed the hood, and yanked it down.

Louise and Charlie let out gasps at the same time.

"Hello, Kevin," said Frankie.

CHAPTER 8

Frankie's brother stared back at him.

"What's he doing here?" asked Max.

"Are you *talking*?" said Kevin.

"That's right, mister," said Max. "And I asked you a question."

"You two know each other?" said Prince Egbert.

"We're brothers," said Frankie and Kevin together.

Kevin folded his arms, grumpily. "I came back to the classroom just after I kicked the ball," he said. "I thought I should apologize, y'know, for wrecking your silly model. Then I found the doorway, or whatever it is. I *knew* there was something weird about that old soccer ball of yours."

Frankie glared at his brother. "It's none of your business."

Kevin gave a hollow laugh. "We'll see about that."

The Ref stepped between them. He was holding the Crone's staff, now dripping with doggy saliva.

"Sorry to interrupt," he said,
"but I think we've had enough
of squabbling brothers in this
kingdom. It's time for you to go
home."

With a wave of his staff, Kevin
disappeared. Frankie felt himself
fading, too. As he vanished, his

final sight was Arthur and Egbert, shaking hands.

Then he was back in the classroom, holding the magic soccer ball, standing with Charlie and Louise.

And, unfortunately, Kevin.

"That was so cool," said Kevin, a wicked glint in his eye. He reached out to snatch the soccer ball, but Frankie kept hold of it.

"Give it to me!" said Kevin.

"It's mine!" said Frankie.

"What's all the shouting about?" said Mr. Donald, striding angrily through the door. "Kevin, let go of Frankie's ball. Why are you in here, anyway?"

Kevin mumbled something about spare house keys.

"Well, get moving then," said Mr. Donald. As Kevin shuffled out, he cast one last glance at his brother. *Something tells me this argument isn't over*, thought Frankie.

Mr. Donald shook his head. "And Frankie, I've told you before. No balls in the classroom. Now have you finished your project? I need to lock the classroom door."

Frankie turned to the side, so his teacher could see the broken model. He wondered how on earth he was going to explain the mess.

"Well, that is spectacular!" said
Mr. Donald.

Louise laughed.

Frankie looked up and couldn't
believe what he was seeing. Not
only was the model whole, but it
looked even better than before.
The drawbridge was half-lowered
on a pulley system. Silk flags flew
from the poles, and there was
even a model stable in the castle
courtyard, with a miniature horse
trough.

"That extra time was definitely
worth it," said Charlie, grinning
from ear to ear.

"A-plus!" said Mr. Donald, "but

what's that?" He peered closer,
taking one of the flags between his
fingertips. Frankie saw it had three
letters on it.

"What's FFC?" said Mr. Donald.
"It doesn't sound very medieval."

Frankie looked at Charlie and
Louise and the three of them burst
out laughing.

"Should we go in, too?" Frankie asked. "Maybe Louise got lost."

"Nah," said Charlie, glancing toward the haunted house. "She'll be out soon."

Frankie and Charlie were standing by the exit, waiting for their friend Louise. The sun was dropping behind the Ferris wheel, and soon the carnival would be shutting down for the year and leaving town.

"Not scared, are you?" said Frankie.

Charlie blushed, and all his freckles stood out. "Of course not."

Frankie grinned. He remembered that Charlie hadn't wanted to go in last year, either. It *was* pretty scary. There were walking skeletons, dangling spiders, and wailing ghosts. He would have gone in again today with Louise, but it cost a dollar and he only had fifty cents left.